TRANSFORMERS

FORMERS

P R I M E

Little, Brown and Company

Hachette Book Group
237 Park Avenue, New York, NY 10017
Visit our website at www.lb-kids.com

Little, Brown and Company is a division of Hachette Book Group, Inc.
The Little, Brown name and logo are trademarks of Hachette Book Group, Inc.

The publisher is not responsible for websites (or their content)
that are not owned by the publisher.

First Edition: May 2013

ISBN 978-0-316-18875-3

10 9 8 7 6 5 4 3

Library of Congress Control Number: 2012942814

CWM

Printed in the United States of America

LICENSED BY:

OPTIMUS PRIME and the SECRET MISSION

Adapted by Ray Santos
Based on the episode "Convoy"
written by Joseph Kuhr

LITTLE, BROWN AND COMPANY
New York Boston

Optimus Prime and his team of Autobots have been living on Earth, protecting humans from the evil Decepticons. Today, the U.S. government gives them a secret mission for national security.

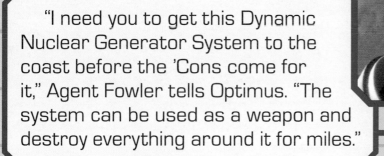

"I need you to get this Dynamic Nuclear Generator System to the coast before the 'Cons come for it," Agent Fowler tells Optimus. "The system can be used as a weapon and destroy everything around it for miles."

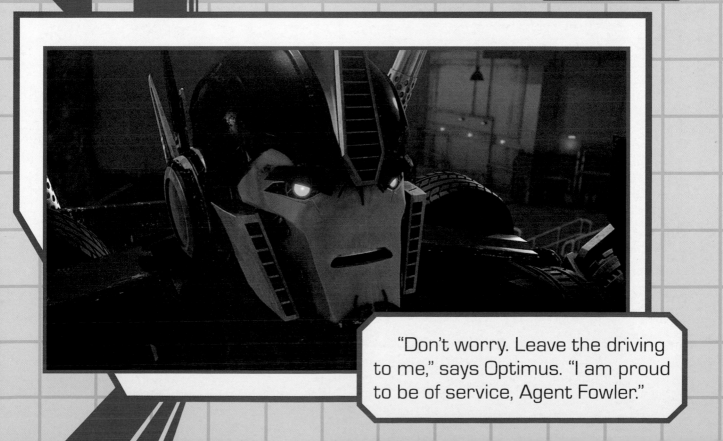

"Don't worry. Leave the driving to me," says Optimus. "I am proud to be of service, Agent Fowler."

Optimus Prime assembles his Autobot team of Arcee, Bulkhead, and Bumblebee to set out on the top secret mission. "Autobots, roll out!"

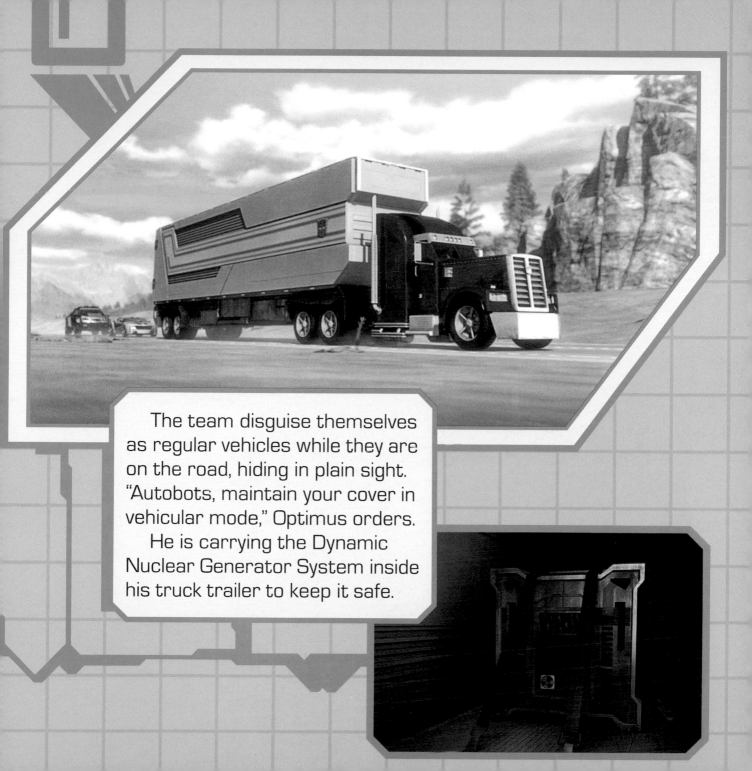

The team disguise themselves as regular vehicles while they are on the road, hiding in plain sight. "Autobots, maintain your cover in vehicular mode," Optimus orders.

He is carrying the Dynamic Nuclear Generator System inside his truck trailer to keep it safe.

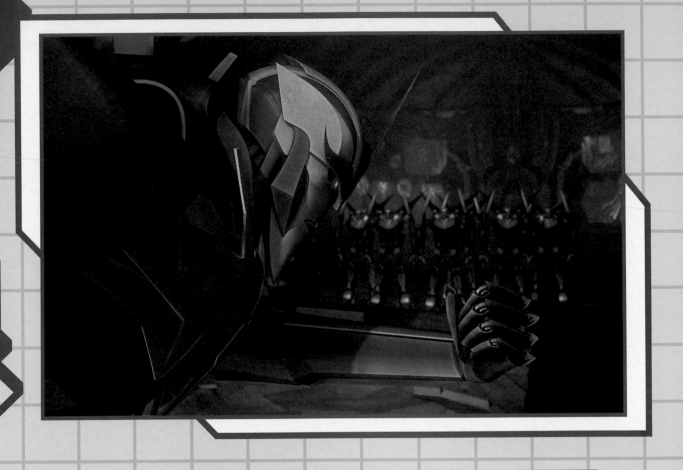

Agent Fowler was right. The Decepticons want the Dynamic Nuclear Generator System—and they want to use it as the ultimate weapon.

Starscream tracks the Autobot convoy and sends a group of Decepticons to steal it! "Find those Autobots and scrap them!" he tells his troopers.

"Yes, Lord Starscream!" they cry.

Like Starscream, these Decepticons can change form. They become powerful jets.

The 'Cons set off and scope out the road from the air, looking for Optimus and his team.

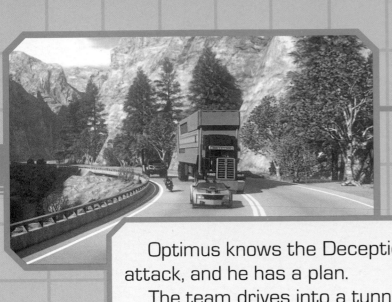

Optimus knows the Decepticons will probably attack, and he has a plan.

The team drives into a tunnel to get out of sight. Bumblebee and Bulkhead shift forms. They remove the secret power source from Optimus's trailer and hide it on a train.

It's the last place the Decepticons will look for it!

After hiding the Dynamic Nuclear Generator System, the Autobots change back into vehicles and zoom out of the tunnel to continue their drive to the coast.

They hide the power source just in time. Starscream's troopers swoop down and land in their path.
The Autobots change into their robot forms for battle.

"After a long car trip, it feels good to get out, stretch my legs, and kick some tailpipe," Bulkhead says, pounding his fists. He is always ready for a fight and doesn't like staying in car mode for too long.

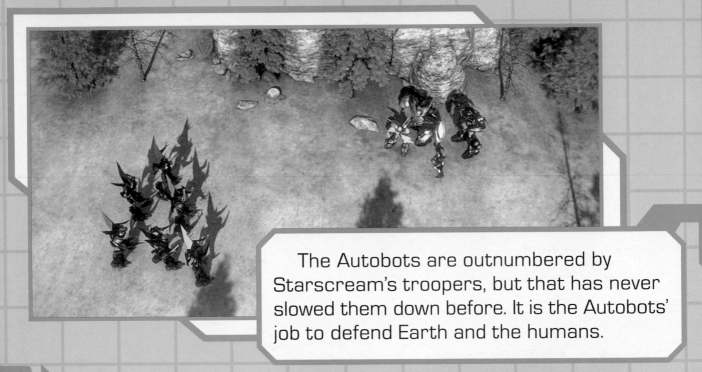

The Autobots are outnumbered by Starscream's troopers, but that has never slowed them down before. It is the Autobots' job to defend Earth and the humans.

Sparks fly as the Decepticon troopers attack. Optimus takes down several with a sweep of his powerful arm.

The smaller Bumblebee moves fast and takes care of several enemies, while Arcee dodges blows and returns a few of her own.

Bulkhead is a wrecking machine. His mighty form plows right through a team of Decepticons.

Optimus worries that he can't keep the train a secret for much longer. The Decepticons will figure out soon enough that the Autobots don't have the Dynamic Nuclear Generator System with them.

He hates leaving his friends in the middle of a battle, but he knows that he has to protect the train. What should he do?

Before Optimus can make up his mind, he hears a giant explosion in the distance. A Decepticon missile has blown apart the tracks ahead of the train!

Optimus has no choice but to leave his friends and try to stop the train. If the train derails, the potential weapon will certainly explode and destroy everything for miles. He takes off at a run.

Meanwhile, the team finally defeats Starscream's troopers and leaves them in a heap.

Arcee looks around. "Hey, where is Optimus?" she asks.

Bulkhead gestures in the direction of the train tracks. "He had a train to catch!" he says. "Come on. Let's go see if he needs help."

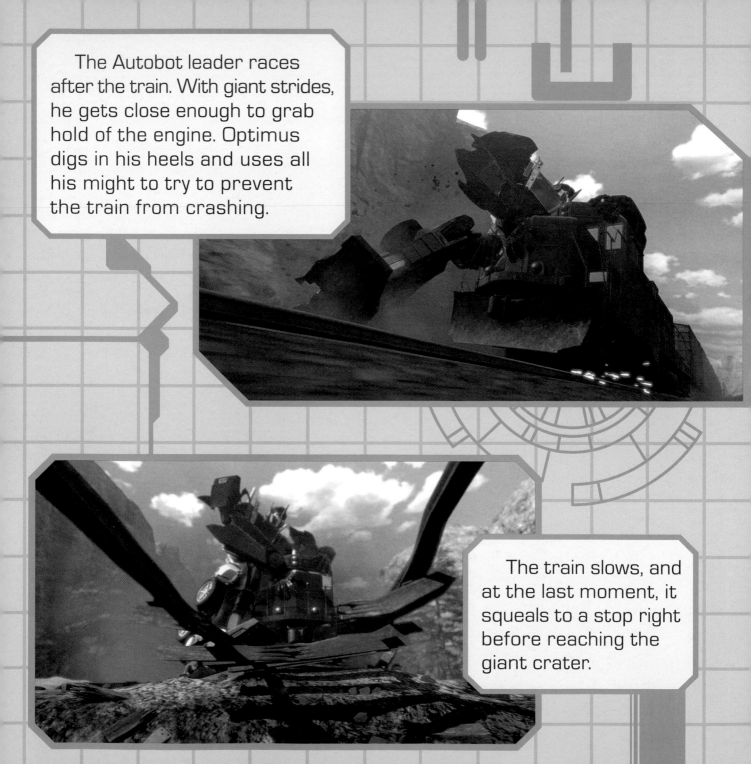

The Autobot leader races after the train. With giant strides, he gets close enough to grab hold of the engine. Optimus digs in his heels and uses all his might to try to prevent the train from crashing.

The train slows, and at the last moment, it squeals to a stop right before reaching the giant crater.

Bumblebee, Bulkhead, and Arcee arrive just in time to see their boss save the day.

The Dynamic Nuclear Generator System is safe, and the Decepticons are defeated. But Optimus and the Autobots know that even though this secret mission is almost complete, there is likely another one waiting for them.

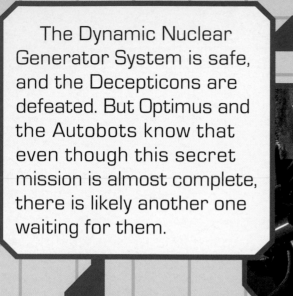

"Autobots, roll out!" Optimus calls to his friends.